THIS LITTLE PIRATE

This Little Pirate

by PHILEMON STURGES

illustrated by AMY WALROD

PUFFIN BOOKS

To Donna Brooks, an amazing editor who taught me how
to make hens cluck, dogs sniff, and pigs celebrate!
—P.S.

For Little Lucas, with love.
And special thanks to Amiko, who kept me smiling
and laughing on my desert island.
—A.W.

PUFFIN BOOKS
Published by the Penguin Group
Penguin Young Readers Group, 345 Hudson Street, New York, New York 10014, USA
Penguin Group (Canada), 90 Eglinton Avenue East, Suite 700, Toronto, Ontario, Canada M4P 2Y3
(a division of Pearson Penguin Canada Inc)
Penguin Books Ltd, 80 Strand, London WC2R 0RL, England
Penguin Ireland, 25 St Stephen's Green, Dublin 2, Ireland
(a division of Penguin Books Ltd)
Penguin Group (Australia), 250 Camberwell Road, Camberwell, Victoria 3124, Australia
(a division of Pearson Australia Group Pty Ltd)
Penguin Books India Pvt Ltd, 11 Community Centre, Panchsheel Park, New Delhi - 110 017, India
Penguin Group (NZ), Cnr Airborne and Rosedale Roads, Albany, Auckland 1310, New Zealand
(a division of Pearson New Zealand Ltd)
Penguin Books (South Africa) (Pty) Ltd, 24 Sturdee Avenue, Rosebank, Johannesburg 2196, South Africa

Registered Offices: Penguin Books Ltd, 80 Strand, London WC2R 0RL, England

First published in the United States of America by Dutton Children's Books,
a division of Penguin Young Readers Group, 2005
Published by Puffin Books, a division of Penguin Young Readers Group, 2007

10 9 8 7 6 5 4 3 2 1

Text copyright © Philemon Sturges, 2005
Illustrations copyright © Amy Walrod, 2005
All rights reserved

THE LIBRARY OF CONGRESS HAS CATALOGED THE DUTTON CHILDREN'S BOOKS EDITION AS FOLLOWS:
Sturges, Philemon
This little pirate / by Philemon Sturges ; illustrated by Amy Walrod—1st ed.
p. cm.
Summary: Two bands of pirates fight over a box, but when they raise the white flag
and open the box together, they find a treasure to share.
ISBN: 0-525-46440-9 (hardcover)
[1. Pirates—Fiction 2. Buried treasure—Fiction 3. Parties—Fiction 4. Pigs—Fiction 5. Stories in rhyme]
I. Walrod, Amy, ill. II. Title
PZ8.3.S9227Th 2005
[E]—dc22 2004020907
Puffin Books ISBN 978-0-14-240850-6
Manufactured in China

This little pirate
spied the island.

This little pirate
saw the rocks.

This little pirate
dropped the anchor,

and this little pirate
found the box.

Then this big pirate yelled, "Yo-ho-ho!
The box is ours and home we'll go!"

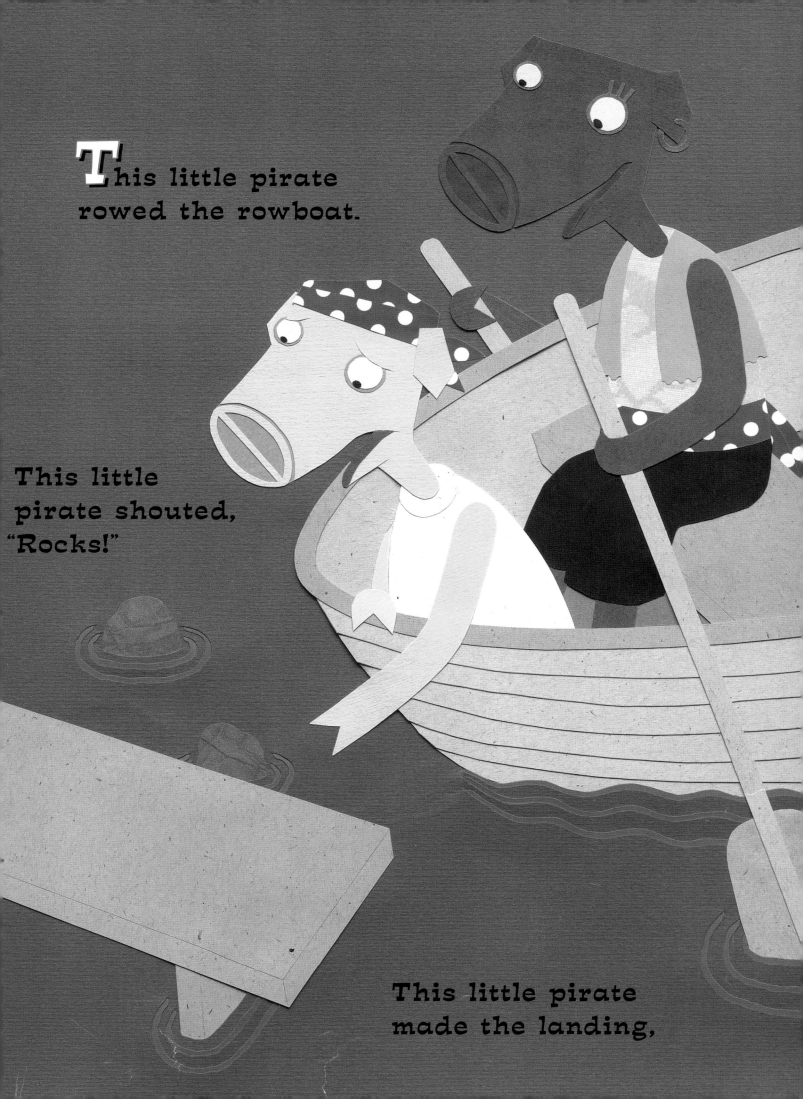

This little pirate
rowed the rowboat.

This little
pirate shouted,
"Rocks!"

This little pirate
made the landing,

and this little pirate hollered, "Box!"

Then this big pirate yelled, "Yo-ho-ho!
This box is *ours*, and home *you'll* go!"

Then those ten rowdy pirates
wrestled and whooped

till they were all *completely...*

Then this big pirate waved a white truce flag,
and this big pirate did, too.
"Why don't we try to open the top?"
asked the exasperated crew.

So four little pirates found a rope,

and four more climbed a tree.

Then the two big pirates tied a secret knot,

and they all pulled—one, two, THREE!

The top popped off, and they looked inside.
"It's party stuff!" those pirates cried.

So these little pirates baked a great big cake,

and these little pirates made spoons.

These clever pirates made enormous hats,

and these puffing pirates filled balloons.

Those ten hungry pirates all ate like pigs—
They burp-slurp-gobble-guzzled fast.
Then they grabbed their presents—
"OH, WOW!" they roared.
"Let's have a mighty pirate BLAST!"

So this little pirate blew his trumpet,

and this one banged her drum.

This mellow pirate played his saxophone,

and this one hummed a hum.

This proud pirate
puffed her tuba.

This pirate
whacked her gong.

This cool pirate
slid his big trombone,

and this pirate
sang a song.

The two big pirates just jigged all about
till the sun went down and the stars came out.

When the red crab ate the last cookie
and the fat clam polished off the cake,
the eight little pirates discovered
that they just couldn't stay awake.

So these tired pirates
rowed to the boats

while these drowsy pirates
watched for rocks.

As these sleepy pirates
set the towline,

these groggy pirates stowed th box

Then these weary pirates put on jammies.

These worn-out pirates said, " 'Night."

As these tuckered pirates hugged teddies,

these pooped pirates slept tight.

But the two big pirates stayed up till dawn
with nary a nod and not one yawn.
And they sang as they sailed 'neath the starry dome,
"Yo-ho-ho!
Ho-ho-ho!"

All the way home!